Picasso-ville

An imaginary place consisting of the visions of *Pablo Picasso*.

Written & Illustrated by Pat Luttrell ~ Inspired by Pablo Picasso

Picasso-ville
is dedicated to my loving family.
My sincere appreciation and gratitude
for constantly encouraging me, believing in me,
and listening to all of my crazy ideas and dreams.

A special thank you to my many friends and colleagues
for sharing their wisdom and kind words.

I am so truly blessed!

> "Everything you can imagine is real."
> **PABLO PICASSO**

Copyright © 2014 by Pat Luttrell
All rights reserved
This book, or parts thereof, may not be reproduced or publicity
performed in any form without written permission of the publisher.
JH Books

Printed in the United States of America

ISBN-13: 978-1494319960

I remember falling fast asleep
with my pup upon my lap.
So many winding roads ahead,
I wished I had a map.

**Juan-les-Pins. 1920. Oil on canvas.
Pablo Picasso**

The roads are straight and yet they curve.
Each led to Picasso Square,
Where people gather to say hello.
There sat a girl with pretty green hair.

Say hello to a Cavalier.

**Girl with a Boat (Maya Picasso).
1938. Oil on canvas.
Pablo Picasso**

**Cavalier with Pipe. 1968.
Oil on canvas.
Pablo Picasso**

I wish I had an ice cream cone!

Man with a Straw Hat and Ice Cream Cone. 1938. Oil on canvas. Pablo Picasso

I'll hold on to the music.

The sound of music filled the air,
As three musicians came into sight.
One played a flute, another guitar.
One holding music stood on the right.

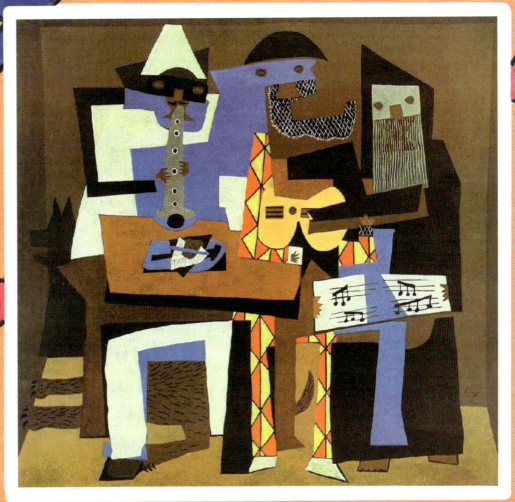

**Three Musicians. 1921 Oil on canvas.
Pablo Picasso**

These ruffles are itchy.

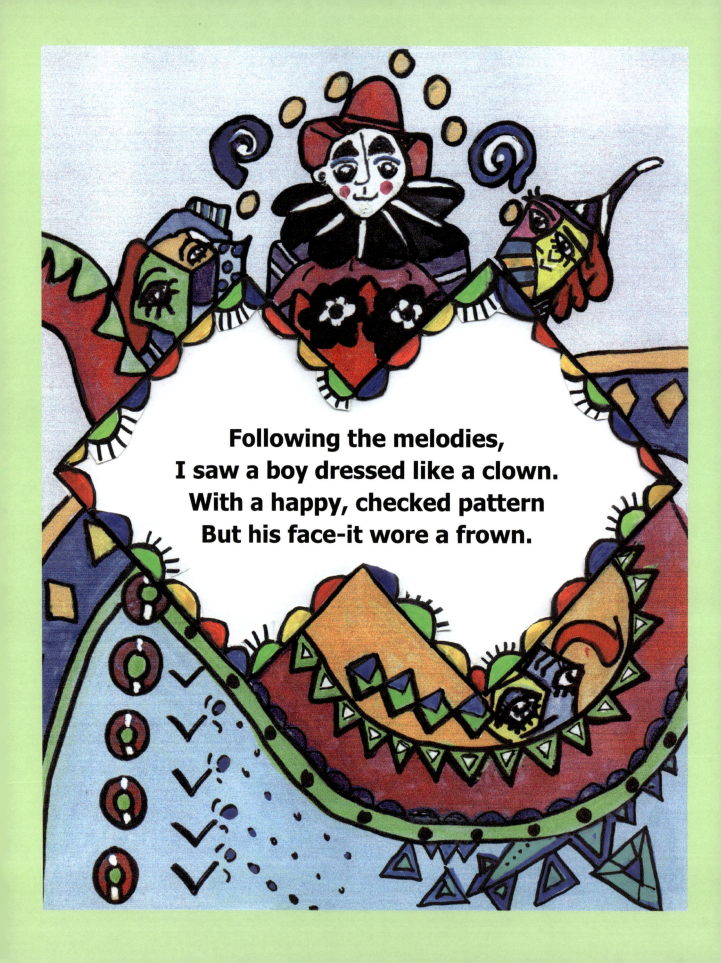

Following the melodies,
I saw a boy dressed like a clown.
With a happy, checked pattern
But his face-it wore a frown.

**Paulo, Picasso's Son, as Harlequin.
1924. Oil on canvas.
Pablo Picasso**

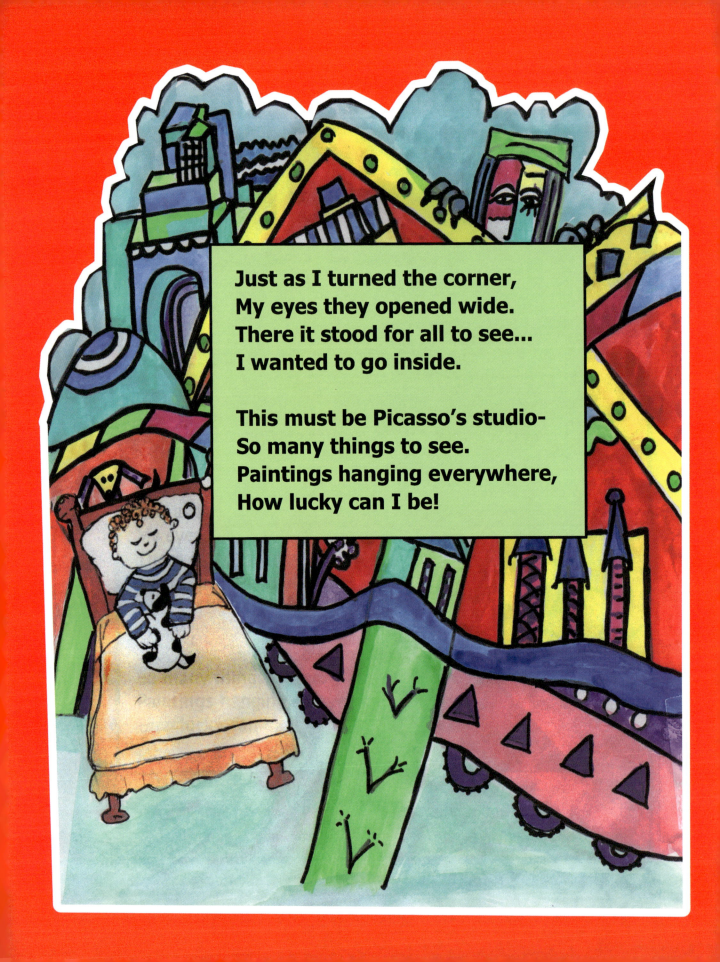

Just as I turned the corner,
My eyes they opened wide.
There it stood for all to see...
I wanted to go inside.

This must be Picasso's studio-
So many things to see.
Paintings hanging everywhere,
How lucky can I be!

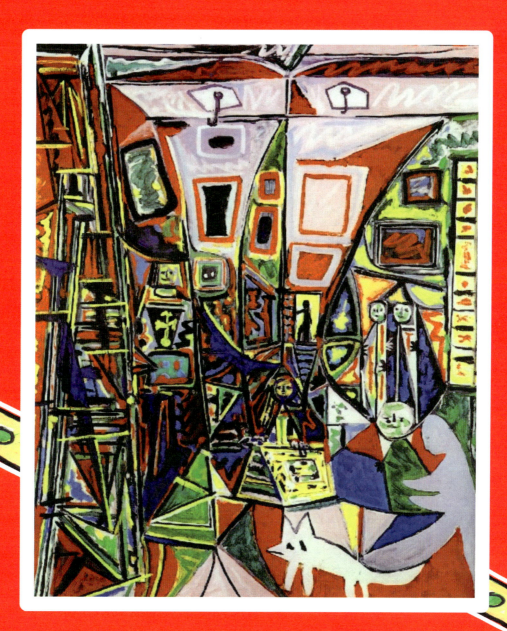

**Meninas after Velasquez.
1957. Oil on canvas.
Pablo Picasso**

It's nice to meet you- I'm Picasso!

There he was the
great Picasso,
Staring right at me.
My heart was beating,
oh so quickly,
What could this feeling be?

The greatest artist
ever born-
has invited me to see,
His many works of art
and more
Now can this really
be?

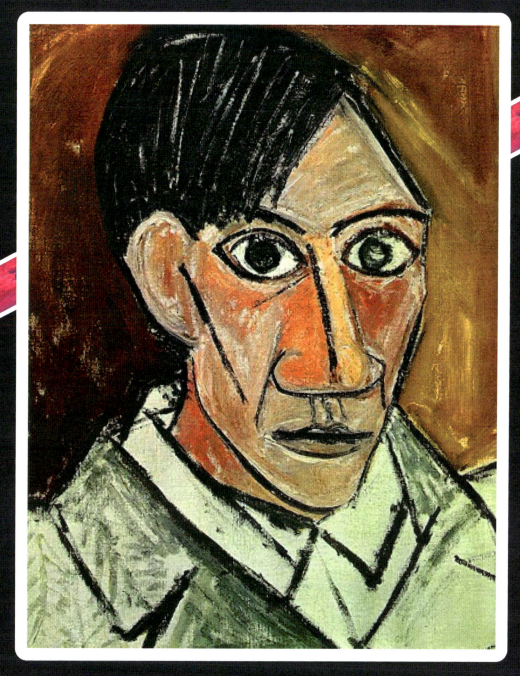

**Self-Portrait. 1907. Oil on canvas.
Pablo Picasso**

Wake up and smell the flowers!

**Dove of Peace. 1949.
Lithograph.
Pablo Picasso**

I woke up so excited!
My dream it seemed so real.
Picasso-ville was magical-
In the way it made me feel.

**I remember seeing Picasso
draw a dove with big white wings.
He said to me
"To draw you must close your eyes and sing."**

**I really loved Picasso-ville- It's like a dream come true.
I love to draw and paint and sing,
I must be an artist too!**

"I paint objects as I think them,
not as I see them."
Pablo Picasso

Juan-les-Pins. 1920. Oil on canvas.
Private Collection

Girl with a Boat (Maya Picasso). 1938.
Oil on canvas.
Galerie Rosengart, Lucerne, Switzerland

Cavalier with Pipe. 1968.
Oil on canvas.
Galerie Rosengart, Lucerne, Switzerland

Man with a Straw Hat and Ice Cream Cone.
1938. Oil on canvas.
Musee Picasso, Paris France

Three Musicians. 1921. Oil on canvas.
Museum of Modern Art, NY, NY

Paulo, Picasso's Son, as Harlequin.
1924. Oil on canvas.
Musee Picasso, Paris France

Meninas after Velasquez, 1957.
Oil on canvas.
Barcelona, Picasso Museum

Self Portrait. 1907. Oil on canvas.
Narodni Gallery, Prague, Czech Republic

Dove of Peace. 1949. Lithograph.
Private Collection

"To draw you must close your eyes and sing." **Pablo Picasso**

Hand with Bouquet. 1930

He was born October 25, 1881 in Malaga, Spain and by the time he died in France in April of 1973, had created a staggering 22,000 works of art in a variety of mediums, including sculpture, ceramics, mosaics, stage design and graphic arts. Pablo Picasso demonstrated uncanny artistic talent in his early years, painting in a realistic manner through his childhood and adolescence; during the first decade of the twentieth century his style changed as he experimented with different theories, techniques, and ideas.

As critic Robert Hughes (Time Magazine) noted, "There was scarcely a 20th century movement that he didn't inspire, contribute to or--in the case of Cubism, which, in one of art history's great collaborations, he co-invented with Georges Braque--beget." Quite simply, as well as being a force of culture, Picasso was also a force of nature. His revolutionary artistic accomplishments brought him universal renown and immense fortune throughout his life, making him one of the best known figures in twentieth century art.

Made in the USA
Charleston, SC
18 May 2014